Mountains, Monsoons, and Mules

By Alicia Klepeis

Illustrated by Simon Abbott

Rourke
Educational Media
rourkeeducationalmedia.com

www.rourkeeducationalmedia.com

Edited by: Keli Sipperley
Cover and Interior layout by: Renee Brady
Cover and Interior Illustrations by: Simon Abbott

Library of Congress PCN Data

Mountains, Monsoons, and Mules / Alicia Klepeis
(Rourke's World Adventures Chapter Books)
ISBN (hard cover)(alk. paper) 978-1-63430-398-9
ISBN (soft cover) 978-1-63430-498-6
ISBN (e-Book) 978-1-63430-592-1
Library of Congress Control Number: 2015933798

Printed in the United States of America,
North Mankato, Minnesota

Dear Parents and Teachers:

Rourke's Adventure Chapter Books engage readers immediately by grabbing their attention with exciting plots and adventurous characters.

Our Adventure Chapter Books offer longer, more complex sentences and chapters. With minimal illustrations, readers must rely on the descriptive text to understand the setting, characters, and plot of the book. Each book contains several detailed episodes all centered on a single plot that will challenge the reader.

Each adventure book dives into a country. Readers are not only invited to tag along for the adventure but will encounter the most memorable monuments and places, culture, and history. As the characters venture throughout the country, they address topics of family, friendship, and growing up in a way that the reader can relate to.

Whether readers are reading the books independently or you are reading with them, engaging with them after they have read the book is still important. We've included several activities at the end of each book to make this both fun and educational.

Are you ready for this adventure?

Enjoy,
Rourke Educational Media

Table of Contents

Better Than Summer Camp (Except the Shots)

"Man, this weather is totally gross! It's been pouring all week." Ten-year-old Anara complained to her twin sister, Samal, on their bus ride home from dance class.

"I know. And one of my rain boots has a slice in the side so my feet are sopping. I can't wait to throw on some dry clothes and fuzzy socks."

After clomping up the three flights of stairs to their apartment, the girls found their eight-year-old brother, Oliver, sprawled across the carpet. He was in the middle of a massive Lego game. They dropped their backpacks loudly on the kitchen floor. "Shh," Ollie said. "Mom's on a work call."

The girls dashed to their room to put on dry clothes before the after-school feeding frenzy began. Samal threw on her flamingo onesie, complete with a beak on the hood and palm tree zipper pull. As

always, Samal had a bowl of cereal with almond milk. And Anara made peanut butter toast and a vanilla milkshake. Sitting at the kitchen counter, the twins started discussing their summer plans. Ever since their parents got divorced, they usually spent most of July with Dad. Then they went to camp for a chunk of August.

Oliver, however, wasn't a big fan of sleepaway camp. Last year he picked a construction-themed camp in Brooklyn near Dad's apartment. He'd built a skateboard and a shelf to keep his toy soldier collection on.

Anara hoped to go back to drama camp in the Adirondacks. Last year she'd had a blast playing Tweedledum in the camp's production of Alice in Wonderland. Samal wanted to try an art and architecture program called ArtVentures! Art Camp. Anara rolled her eyes at Samal, "You're such a nerd, Sam. You are seriously like the only ten-year-old with a subscription to Architectural Digest."

Samal looked offended. Anara patted her sister on the back. "Just kidding. It sounds right up your alley."

Just then, Mom came out of her office. Actually, it was really just a desk and a file cabinet in the corner of her bedroom. The girls thought she looked kind of flushed, but neither of them said anything.

Over their breakfast-for-dinner meal, Mom told the kids that she had some interesting news. "My boss, Dr. Williamson, called last night. He's got another assignment for me. I have to go to India for a couple of weeks in August."

Mom regularly traveled for work. She worked for a branch of the UN called UNESCO, the United Nations Educational, Scientific and Cultural Organization. She often led teams of people to ensure that various natural and cultural sites around the world were being taken care of properly. But she really enjoyed trying to establish new sites.

"Are we going to stay with Dad?" Ollie asked. That was normally how it worked when Mom had a travel assignment. But this year had been really unusual. They'd gone with Mom to Egypt in October and Italy in February.

"Well, there are a few possibilities. Dad says we could switch our usual summer arrangement so you could stay with me in July and go to him and/or camp in August. Or…" she kept quiet for dramatic effect, "Vovó says she could meet us in India and hang out with you while I'm at work."

All three kids started squealing with delight. Vovó was Dad's mother. She lived outside of Helsinki, Finland's capital city. A couple of summers ago, Vovó took Anara, Samal, and Ollie hiking and biking in Acadia National Park. They'd had a great time.

Mom's eyes were crinkling up at the corners, which meant she was happy. "I take it your squeals mean you'd rather skip camp and go to India, eh? It will probably cost less money to travel in India than go to camp, crazily enough." The girls had noticed that Mom definitely worried more about money since she and Dad split up. They worried some, too.

"By the way, did I hear some complaining about the rain? I should warn you that the timing of this India trip was not my choice. It's going to be monsoon season in August. Are you sure you're still up for it?" Mom teased.

The kids confirmed that crummy weather was not going to stop them from meeting up with Vovó.

They'd absolutely brave the elements, they said, though fashion-forward Samal was quick to suggest that they now had the perfect excuse to get new rain boots and jackets.

Over April break, the twins began helping with some of the trip planning. They had fun reading about cool things like unusual flavors of ice cream and buildings like the Taj Mahal. They discovered that they'd be in India for Independence Day. But Anara and Samal were horrified when they looked at the Center for Disease Control website. They were going to need medicine or shots for Hepatitis A, Typhoid, Japanese encephalitis, *and* Malaria. Bummer!

Gearing Up and Future Contacts

The time flew by between April vacation and the August India trip. Oliver passed his yellow belt test in karate; the girls had their end-of-the-year dance recital; and all three kids advanced another level in their swim lessons. While Mom traveled to Morocco and Papua New Guinea, Anara, Samal, and Ollie stayed with Dad.

The week before the trip, the Nylunds' apartment looked like a tornado had blown through. Piles of stuff lay everywhere. Anara commented that Mom's backpack looked like a traveling pharmacy. Besides oodles of hand sanitizer and Ollie's EpiPen, they'd bought bed nets to prevent mosquito bites, water purification tablets, insect bite treatment, and altitude sickness medicine. Ollie's favorite purchase was the anti-diarrhea medicine because it gave him the excuse to say "diarrhea" and talk about poop even more than usual.

Not counting boring stuff like toiletries, here's what made the India packing list:

India Packing List

Rain gear
Short pajamas or cotton nightgowns
Sneakers and sandals
Hiking boots
Shorts and T-shirts
Cotton sundresses
Underwear and socks
Pants
Small backpacks to hold entertainment stuff
Journals
Activities/Toys for plane
Archidoodle: The Architect's Activity Book
(Samal)
Digital camera
Pens, colored pencils, markers
Sketchpad
Stuffed animals (Samal – rainbow chameleon;
Anara – elephant; Oliver – buffalo)

One of the twins' jobs was to check the weight of each bag they'd packed on the scale. They'd been warned not to pack stuff they didn't really need. Their trips to Egypt and Italy had taught them that moving from place to place was much harder with heavy bags.

Ollie's bags were all pretty light. Besides his clothes, he'd added very little—a few toy soldiers, a yoyo, and some Star Wars cards. When Anara picked up Samal's suitcase, she groaned. "Holy cow, Samal, did you pack bricks? This thing weighs a ton!"

"Holy cow—that's a good one, Anara. Did you know cows are sacred in India? I just read that somewhere. Anyway, I wanted to have plenty of outfits. You never know where we'll be going. Don't you think having more undies and socks is probably a good idea? The average August temperature in Delhi is about ninety degrees."

"Ew," Anara complained. "It's going to be insanely hot and sticky, isn't it? But that bag of yours is not heavy with just undies and socks. Mom will kill you if your bag is overweight. You get fined for that."

"I heard that," Mom said. "And monsoon-season

India is definitely a place where good deodorant is in order."

"Yuck!" Samal was not a fan of smelly people. She got enough of them riding the buses and trains between Brooklyn and Queens every summer.

The kids loved the day before departure. Dad took the day off and outfitted them with books, fancy flavors of sugarless gum, and gift cards so they could download new music and games on the iPad they shared.

With the packing done, Mom and the kids headed to Pari's house. Pari was the twins' best friend from school. Samal thought Pari had the coolest name ever because it meant "fairy." Pari's mom, Charu, offered to host the Nylunds for dinner since their fridge was empty. As soon as they walked in the door, Pari's younger brother Fazel grabbed Ollie to go play.

Charu gave Mom and the girls tons of ideas of places to see on their trip. She'd also made a list of their relatives living in various parts of India. Charu told Mom that all of them would be looking out for a possible call or email from her. They would be delighted to host Pari's friends, she told them.

When it was time to go, Charu taught them to say "Namaste" instead of goodbye.

Finally the Nylunds made their way to New York's JFK Airport. They spent the next fourteen hours aboard Air India's Flight 102, nonstop from New York to New Delhi–a journey of over 7,000 miles.

Dramas and Diversion in Delhi

Leaving the air-conditioned comfort of Indira Gandhi International Airport was a shock to the system. The Nylunds headed out onto the sidewalk to the taxi stand. "Holy moly!" Samal spluttered. "I feel like I'm inside a dryer full of steaming, still-wet laundry. How hot is it here?"

Ollie noticed an electronic sign nearby. "About 34 degrees Celsius. What's that in our temperature? I don't know Celsius."

Using temperature conversion app on Mom's phone to convert to Fahrenheit, Anara replied, "In the low 90s. The forecast said it was supposed to rain today. I hope it does. It's gross out now."

They loaded their bags into the first cab to pull up. Unlike the all-yellow hybrid taxis in New York, this one was kind of ancient-looking. It reminded Ollie of the character Doc Hudson from the movie *Cars*.

Unfortunately, the taxi driver also drove his vehicle like it was a racecar. He seemed to have only one speed–fast. As he wove in and out of the six lanes of traffic, all four Nylunds felt like they might throw up. Mom asked the driver to slow down, but he just waved his hand at her dismissively.

About twenty minutes into the ride, the inevitable happened. In his excessive speed and weaving, the driver had not seen a bicyclist on the side of the road. Screech went the tires and then Crash! "Oh no! We didn't hit that man, did we?" Anara clutched onto Mom, fearing the worst.

"No, love. We definitely didn't hit him." Swerving to just barely miss the man on the bike, the taxi driver crashed into a guardrail, though not at top speed. "Is everyone okay?" Mom asked. The kids all nodded, though they felt a bit shaken up. The driver was raging on and swearing like a mad man. The car was now unable to be driven, thanks to two flat tires and a seriously bent right fender. Mom asked him to open the trunk and everyone took their bags out.

Luckily, within moments, another taxi driver came by. Seeing their plight, he picked them up and apologized for their bad start. "Not all Delhi drivers are like that one," he said. "I'll get you where you want to go in one piece." All four Nylunds nodded gratefully.

Once they were safely inside the hotel lobby, Oliver said he still felt kind of sick to his stomach. On a positive note, since Mom had lots of meetings at UNESCO's Delhi office, the UN had put them up in a pretty fancy hotel for the next few days.

After their stressful journey, Mom really wanted to go find some decent food. But her plan went awry when the man at the reception desk mentioned the outdoor pool.

"Please, pretty please? Can we swim a little, Mom?" Oliver asked.

"Okay, okay," Mom relented. "But only a thirty minute swim if there's no lightning out." The twins and Ollie wore their rash guards so they didn't have to get totally slathered in sunscreen. Having fair skin meant sunburns were easy to get, even in just a short time. But splashing around and taking turns on the pool's spiral slide boosted everyone's spirits.

Later, sporting their new sundresses, the girls felt

stylish for their late afternoon outing. As identical twins, Anara and Samal refused to wear outfits that were too similar. When they were little, people always bought them matching stuff. They both disliked dressing the same, especially fashionista Samal. She always said to Anara, "I may have your face, but I don't need your wardrobe too."

After their hairy cab ride, Anara insisted on walking to Connaught Place, their dinner destination. "Besides." she noted, "I'd rather get some fresh air."

Ollie quipped, "This humid air does not feel fresh to me. I'd have taken any air-conditioned vehicle around."

Mom rolled her eyes. "Fresh is a relative term, Oliver."

All the cool stores in the mall tempted Anara. "Can we go in this shop, Mom? I really like that scarf. I have some money left from my birthday."

"If you start shopping this early in the trip, you'll never fit everything in your bags by the end. Sorry, babe." Anara sulked for a few minutes but decided to let it go. She decided to put her energy into helping her siblings choose a restaurant.

Stopping in front of Punjabi Palace, Samal asked what the difference was between Indian and Punjabi. Surprisingly, map-lover Oliver had her answer. He told her that Punjab was a state in northern India. Ollie was in charge of ordering drinks for their Punjabi Palace meal. He chose lassi, but not the mango kind they had at Pari's house. Punjabi lassi was often quite a simple drink, made by blending yogurt and water and sugar and occasionally other spices. The menu also had a version with salt instead of sugar. "Ew," Anara said. "Who'd want a salty yogurt drink?"

Mom said, "Shh, Anara. One person's sugar is another person's salt. In the hot weather, people often crave salt."

The twins wanted to pick the main courses. Anara chose the matar paneer, a dish consisting of peas and farmer's cheese in a tomato sauce. It came with rice and the flatbread called paratha. Samal wanted to try the dal makhani, made with whole red kidney beans and black lentils, cream and butter.

About two minutes after the food arrived, Samal's face was beet red. Her forehead was sweating–despite the fans in the restaurant. "What's the matter, Sam?"

Ollie asked.

"My mouth is ON FIRE! Quick, order me some water. I'm dying here!" Samal's eyes were wild.

"Remember what Dad said that time he ate a Scotch bonnet pepper by mistake?" Anara asked. "He said milk or bread are the answers. Here, you can have my lassi."

It took about ten minutes for Samal to calm down and stop sweating buckets. She ate all the naan bread on the table and had to order another lassi. Before they left the restaurant, Oliver read some of the fine print at the bottom of the menu. "It says that Punjabi food contains many spices. It recommends requesting extra mild dishes if you don't like your food that way." When Ollie finished reading, all three kids got the giggles.

"I'll definitely remember that in the future," Samal noted.

******

Walking back from dinner, the sky got dark. Crack! Lightning flashed and the skies opened up. It rained like they'd never seen. By the time they made it back to the hotel, they were soaked to the skin. The man behind the reception desk recognized the twins and called them over. He had a message for Mom.

Mom read the note and her face went pale. "Vovó was supposed to arrive tonight but her flight from Helsinki was cancelled due to storms. She is going to show up tomorrow evening instead. What am I going to do? I have loads of meetings tomorrow."

A few minutes later, the hotel manager Arjun made a suggestion. He said that they had an arrangement with another hotel that offered a kids' club. He said he'd check and see if there was any space for childcare. Eventually he came over to where the Nylunds were sitting and said he was able to book three spaces.

Though Mom's face lit up with relief, both Anara and Samal were offended about needing babysitting. "This kids' club thing better not be lame. I don't want to color all day or have to take a nap," Sam complained.

"Hopefully it will have some age-appropriate activities, love. But honestly, I have no choice. Delhi is a mega-city. I can't bring you to ten hours of meetings. You'd be bored out of your tree."

The kids' club turned out to be awesome. There

were fifteen kids altogether. There was a boy named Darren from Ireland and a girl from England named Emma. The four of them had a blast with their director. They made clay pots in the Creative Corner, played tons of video games, and swam in the indoor-outdoor pool with a clear tunnel connecting the two. They also had an hour-long cooking lesson with one of the hotel's chefs and made butter chicken for lunch.

Oliver only had one other kid in his age group, a boy named Alex from California. The boys played video games and played catch in the pool with a special ball that bounced on water. They also had a cooking lesson and made coconut burfi for dessert. Ollie thought the chef said "Barf for dessert," which he thought was hilarious. But it turned out to be yummy. The recipe only had a few ingredients: finely grated coconut, condensed milk, cardamom, and food coloring. The twins agreed it was delicious. They wanted to make it when they got back to New York.

Mom was pleased that their day had been a success. Vovó texted her from the airport to say that she'd made it to New Delhi. Even though Mom and

Dad were divorced, Mom and Vovó got along great. And since Mom's parents were not alive anymore, she was very grateful to have an active grandparent around.

When the twins and Ollie found Vovó in the hotel room, they showered her with hugs and kisses. She'd brought the kids' favorite treats from Finland: salmiakki, a salted licorice, and Marianne candies, which were sweet peppermint shells filled with milk chocolate.

On their first morning together, Ollie asked, "Can we go see the Presidential Palace, Vovó? It's supposed to be close by."

"Yeah, I read about it last night in my book. But I don't think you can go inside, Ollie." Samal told her brother.

"That's okay. It would still be cool to see. It's like the White House in Washington," he said.

It was a short walk to the red sandstone palace known as Rashtrapati Bhavan in Hindi. Through the building's gates, they could see its gardens, classical columns, and some fountains. Anara sketched it in her journal and Samal took some photos for her architecture book.

While the twins were preoccupied, Vovó played a game with Oliver. Skimming Vovó's guidebook, Samal found out that the palace contained 340 rooms and that 29,000 people worked on it at the same time.

Art-lover Anara requested a visit to the National Museum. She was psyched to find out that there was still enough space for her and Samal to take a workshop on Warli painting. "Can we do it, Vovó? It would be awesome to make a painting in India and bring it home."

"Absolutely. I have a secret plan for Ollie," she said mysteriously.

"You mean I don't get to paint with the girls?" Ollie was indignant. He hated being left out of activities because of his age.

"Sorry, handsome. The Warli workshop is for kids over ten. But I happen to know there are some super cool things you'd like to see in the museum."

"Can we do a scavenger hunt?" Oliver remembered doing some in Italy with Vovó. He loved looking for hidden treasures.

"Sounds like a plan," their grandmother said.

The girls looked at the museum's collection of Warli paintings that depicted scenes from daily life. Their teacher said Warli was the name of the largest tribe of people found on the northern outskirts of Mumbai in western India. Anara tried to copy the paintings' style—one color with white designs. Meanwhile, Ollie did a scavenger hunt through the museum. His favorite items were the coin collection and Aurangzeb's Sword, the sword of a 17th century Mughal emperor. It had quotations from the Koran etched onto it.

The Nylunds' last afternoon in Delhi was smelly, hot, and sticky. The rain was nowhere to be seen. Tired of museums and being indoors, Oliver had requested a walk. As they wandered in search of an ice cream shop, Vovó said, "Let's go see a goddess."

Samal said, "What? How can we do that?" All the kids were intrigued. After a few minutes, Anara noticed a funky smell. It wasn't like the exotic spices or sweet mangos from the markets. It was decidedly unpleasant. As Oliver and the twins came upon a river, they found it unlike any river they'd ever seen. It was full of plastic garbage—old water bottles, broken toys, and other junk that no one wanted.

"Where are we?" Ollie asked. "This is the dirtiest river I've ever seen. Why did we come here?"

Vovó stopped in her tracks, looking completely serious. "This is the goddess. The Yamuna River."

Anara was annoyed. She'd been imagining at least a stone statue of some beautiful Indian female deity. "How can a river be a goddess?"

Vovó said people in India worshipped rivers as gods and goddesses. The Yamuna River was the largest branch of India's holy Ganges River. It flowed down from the glaciers of the Himalayan Mountains. The Yamuna once had deep blue water. But pollution from factories and sewage had ruined the water quality so much that today people often described it as a sewer. Fish couldn't even survive in the Delhi part of the river now. And yet people still celebrated holidays and festivals along the Yamuna, even here in Delhi.

Anara later wrote in her journal that she thought Vovó's question was a tease. She didn't want to visit a smelly old river on vacation. She also noted that she was looking forward to spending a little time with Mom before her next meeting in Jaipur.

Train Troubles and the Taj Mahal

The morning after the Yamuna River fiasco, the Nylunds showed up at the New Delhi train station. Its platform was a crazy scene. Porters dashed by carrying trunks, suitcases, even animals in cages for their customers. Ollie was shocked to see a cow having a snooze on the ground in front of the ticket window. "How come no one is shooing him out of the way?" he wondered.

Samal quickly chimed in. "I know this! People in India have great admiration and respect for cows. If a cow passes in front of traffic on a busy road, drivers will wait for it to go by."

Sidestepping the cow, they bought tickets to Agra, their next stop. Commuters and other travelers filled every nook and cranny in sight. Oliver couldn't believe that kids held onto the sides of trains as they departed the station. In the distance they even saw people riding on top of the huge trains. Vovó said it was because not everyone could afford a ticket to ride inside the cars. Anara was horrified to think of what might happen if someone fell off.

As they made their way toward the platform, hundreds of people pushed past them, filling the train before they'd even had a chance to board. They had to wait in a huge line –again– to exchange their tickets after missing the first train. While they waited, some little kids came up and pulled on Anara's skirt. Then they grabbed Samal's water bottle and started tugging the back of her shirt. The twins looked frightened. "Vovó, what do they want? Can we get out of here, please?" Vovó helped Anara and Samal escape from the prying hands.

Once they successfully boarded their first class train to Agra, the girls and Oliver had a lot to say. They peppered Mom and Vovó with questions about the little kids who'd approached them. Samal asked, "Why didn't we give money to them?"

Mom replied calmly, "In my experience, it's better to donate to organizations that work with street children than to the children directly. Sometimes these little kids are made to beg and don't get to buy things they need with the money tourists give them. I understand it can feel mean to not hand out some rupees to these kids. But we'll meet some former street children later on this trip. We'll definitely make a donation to help them then."

It took all three children a while to calm down. Samal said, "I'm going to write in my journal for a while. I want to get my thoughts out on paper before I forget what happened."

"Good idea, Sam. Maybe that'll calm my nerves. That station was freaky." Anara liked her sister's idea and thought some quiet time was definitely in order. After some time journaling and looking out the window, all three kids felt better.

Anara enjoyed walking through the fancy dining car on her way to the bathroom. Sam was delighted when a man came by with spicy, sweet tea called chai. Oliver fell asleep on his Buffalo Bill stuffed animal. He was dead to the world when the train arrived in Agra. Luckily, Agra was the train's last stop. They took a few minutes to collect their belongings so they could avoid the throngs of people departing the train in a hurry.

Just outside the train station, Oliver saw what looked like a bench with a scooter in front of it. "Can we ride in one of those?" he asked.

"What even is that thing?" Anara wondered.

"You guys like the idea of traveling by auto rickshaw, eh?" Vovó queried.

"Auto what?" Ollie asked. "That's one funny looking vehicle."

"Auto rickshaws are the best way to get around Agra if you're willing to live without air conditioning." The kids were always up for an adventure. With all their bags, they hired two of the quirky, brightly painted vehicles. Mom even requested the scenic route so everyone could get a sense of the city. Since it was a Friday, and the Muslim holy day, the Taj Mahal was closed. But Ollie and the girls glimpsed several mosques. They also saw a group of boys playing soccer in a vacant lot. Samal noticed that many shops seemed to be closed for the afternoon.

Finally the rickshaw pulled up in front of a house. Anara was curious. "Why are we stopping here? Isn't this somebody's house?"

"Yep. I booked a homestay with a family in Agra. This way you get to learn about the culture more than in a regular hotel."

"Isn't it weird for people to have strangers staying in their homes?" Samal wondered.

"Not really. It's like a bed-and-breakfast back home. Some people just like hosting others." Vovó said. When they discovered that the owners had left a note saying that they'd be back by 5 p.m., Vovó offered to stay with the bags so others could explore the neighborhood.

About a block away was a tourism office. The kids each grabbed some brochures and maps. Oliver saw an advertisement for the Agra Fort, which of course, Mom had to mention was a UNESCO site.

When they returned to the homestay, they found Vovó having tea with the hostess, Mrs. Akbar. She apologized for not being home when their rickshaw arrived. "Sorry, we had gone to visit some relatives for tiffin after my husband went to pray at the mosque."

Samal asked, "What's tiffin?"

"It's a light meal or snack that people in India enjoy in the late afternoon. It can be sweet or savory.

But it keeps people going until supper. Can I offer you ladies some tea or mango lassi?"

"Yes, please. We love mango lassi!" Anara decided this homestay thing was more fun than a traditional hotel. She thought Mrs. Akbar seemed sweet.

"Your grandma says that you are a history buff, is that right, Oliver?" The tips of Ollie's ears turned pink. "You must go to Agra Fort then. It was the home of many Mughal emperors. The Mughals were members of a Muslim dynasty that ruled much of India from around the sixteenth to the nineteenth centuries. They left their mark on many architectural wonders here in Agra. Of course, you'll also be seeing the most famous one here—the Taj Mahal, right?"

All three kids nodded. Mrs. Akbar quickly popped into the kitchen to make their drinks. With the heat and humidity, it took a lot of restraint not to guzzle them quickly. In a last-minute decision, they decided to visit the fort before the sun set. That way they could just explore the Taj Mahal on their only full day in Agra. Mrs. Akbar's son offered to drop them off in his van since he had to pick up some supplies for their restaurant anyway.

Mom gave Oliver a choice. "Do you want to hire a guide to take us around the fort, Ollie?"

"No, thanks. I'd rather just look around and take some pictures." Not so subtly, the girls breathed a sigh of relief. Samal wanted to do some architectural sketches. Anara brought her sketchpad too.

When they arrived, Samal was surprised by the scene before her. She'd expected cannons and tall walls. But actually the Agra Fort was more of a complex. It had a fortified palace containing royal apartments, mosques, assembly halls and even a dungeon. Anara was shocked that the water running at the fort's base was actually the Yamuna River. It looked much cleaner than the section they'd seen in Delhi.

Before bed, while Samal was writing in her journal, she mentioned how much she liked the fort's red sandstone, especially how the light fell when the sun was setting. She thought it was cool that the fort was crescent-shaped. She'd read somewhere that the crescent was a symbol of Islam and wondered if the fort's shape was deliberately made for that reason. She sketched some of the geometric designs she'd seen in her Archidoodle book.

Mrs. Akbar knocked on the Nylunds' door early the next morning. She'd packed everyone chai in a thermos and parathas stuffed with potatoes, paneer and onions for an Indian breakfast on-the-go. They arrived at the Taj Mahal as the sun was rising. Anara noticed that Vovó was a little teary when they walked up toward the monument. "What's the matter, Vovó? Are you okay?"

"Yes, yes, I'm okay, love. Ukki always wanted to see the Taj Mahal. He was too sick to go the last time we were in India together. But I'm so happy to be here with my grandchildren. I think your Grandpa Ukki is here with everyone in spirit."

Ollie squeezed her hand. The girls hugged her. They hoped he was with them somehow.

Even though it was super-early, the Taj Mahal and its surrounding grounds were far from quiet. People often came either at sunrise or sunset because of the lighting. At sunrise, it had an almost pinkish hue. At midday the brightness of the white marble could be almost blinding.

Their guide Arvind told them, "The Taj Mahal is

a monument to love. Workers began building the monument around 1632. It took seventeen years to finish its construction. The Emperor Shah Jahan built it as a monument to his beloved wife who died after giving birth to their thirteenth child." Anara and Samal gasped at the idea of having thirteen kids.

Oliver said he wished they could swim in the huge lotus pool. Even the girls had to admit that it looked pretty inviting. They visited the museum on the grounds and bought a few souvenirs and postcards to send home to friends.

The next morning, it was back on the rails. This time, however, there was no drama. With Ollie as their unofficial conductor, the group successfully boarded their train to Jaipur. Once on board, it was Samal's turn to ask a teaser question. "Did you know that Jaipur is called the Pink City?" Looking at her siblings, she said, "I'm not telling you why. You'll have to find out for yourselves."

Exploring the Pink City

Anara loved the jumble of modern and old in Jaipur. She was surprised to see camels pulling carts and modern sports cars side-by-side on the city streets. Samal, who had a flair for fashion, admired people's colorful clothes like the ghagharas (skirts), turbans, and jutis (pointed shoes). Women here wore the most vibrant colors—fuchsia, deep orange, and royal purples.

Ollie really wanted to go on a cycle rickshaw ride, where a person bicycles passengers around. So they did. After winding its way past old homes, shops, and even some fort-like structures, the rickshaw dropped them off at Hawa Mahal, aka the Palace of Winds. The five-story-high pink sandstone building quickly became a favorite of Samal's.

Ollie read from a plaque: "This building was called the Palace of the Winds because wind easily passes through the semi-octagonal windows found on every story. The building was deliberately designed so that the ladies of the royal household could watch the city life go by their windows."

"Man, I wish we had windows like that in our apartment," Anara commented. "It's always like an oven in the summer."

"Too true," Samal agreed. "By the way, did you guys notice that on the rickshaw ride here, loads of the buildings were painted pink? Remember my question from the train?"

Anara said, "Yeah, I did, actually." She borrowed Vovó's phone and did a quick Internet search. "Japiur was painted pink when Prince Albert visited India in the mid-nineteenth century. Today there's a law that buildings in Jaipur's Old City must still be painted pink," she read aloud.

The kids got into a debate about what color they would paint their neighborhood if they could only choose one color. Oliver was immediately clear about his selection: green. Samal debated between purple and turquoise but finally settled on purple. Anara said she'd vote for orange, no question. After the kids pressed her to make a decision, Vovó said she'd like canary yellow buildings in her neighborhood.

Instead of taking a vehicle to their next stop, Vovó suggested walking. But the heat of the afternoon was unbearable. Anara was the first to express her displeasure. She wanted a break from being in the middle of zillions of people. Samal's temper was also flaring up. She was a person who definitely needed her down time.

"My brain is hurting. Aren't we supposed to chill out and take a break from learning during summer vacation?" Ollie complained.

Vovó got the message. "Oh, okay, you three. I get the idea. You're a little fried. Travel can do that. Not to mention the horrid heat and humidity today. Let's scrap our original plans and get some kulfi. Then you can go swimming at the hotel."

As they made their way through little alleyways and back streets, Oliver kept pestering Vovó about what kulfi was. She refused to tell him. Just when the twins had enough of Ollie's pestering, they arrived in front of a tiny shop called Pink City Kulfi. Oliver opened the door and nearly fainted with delight.

Between the sweet smell and the air conditioning, they thought they'd found heaven in Jaipur.

Kulfi turned out to be like an Indian version of ice cream. They ordered lots of scoops to share. The frozen dairy dessert was served in little earthenware pots called matka. The girls murmured their delight as they dipped their spoons into containers of rose, mango, elaichi (cardamom), kesar (saffron), and pista (pistachio). There were no rainbow sprinkles but everyone walked away from the shop feeling happier.

Besides cooling off, the Nylund kids were tasked with planning the rest of their agenda in the Pink City. Sitting at a poolside table covered with guidebooks and brochures, Anara let out a squeal. "Oh, my goodness, you guys! Come here!" She told her siblings that people could pay for elephant rides up to the Amber Fort and Palace. Anara's favorite animal in the world was the elephant. She'd had her stuffed animal Ellie since she was a baby. It went everywhere with her.

Over dinner, Mom said it was okay for everyone to ride elephants as long as they followed the guide's directions very carefully. "It's no joke to fall off an elephant," she said.

"Duh!" Anara said.

"That's enough, young lady," Mom chided, shooting a death-ray stare at Anara. "I can just say no to the whole thing."

"Sorry," Anara said, then looked away. Sometimes Anara's sarcastic side got the better of her.

Early the next morning, three excited kids arrived at Amber Fort's parking lot. The line was already long. "The sun is so hot already," Samal complained. "Do you think we'll get a spot to ride? I read that the elephants can only make so many trips in a day."

"I think so, pumpkin. It's still early. I heard the man in front of us say that each elephant can make five trips up the hill per day. The Jaipur government makes sure that the elephants aren't overworked. There are about eighty elephants working here. It looks like each one carries two passengers at a time so I'm optimistic things will work out."

"Can I ride with you, Vovó?" Ollie wanted to know.

Anara begged, "Can we get our picture taken? I want to show my friends at home."

Samal piped in, "Yeah, we always have to write those boring reflections about how we spent our summer vacation at the start of the school year. A photo and story about this would be awesome!"

"That would be great," Vovó agreed.

They waited in line for about an hour. Anara breathed a sigh of relief when the man said his elephants still had a couple more trips up the hill left. The elephant handler helped them climb a stepladder up onto their two elephants. On each elephant's back was a box-like structure to sit in. Anara couldn't get over the beautiful decorations on her elephant's face. Colorful pink, purple, green, and white flowers were painted on its skin.

On the thirty minute walk up the hill, all three children flooded the guide, Varun, with questions. He told them that the elephants they were riding were named Ambara, meaning "sky," and Bala, meaning "young one." He'd gotten Bala as a baby after its mother died in an accident. And Ambara was the first elephant Varun had ridden so he named her for the feeling he had while up in her basket.

As they approached the end of their trip up the hill, Oliver saw something across the path. One of the other elephant handlers was hitting his elephant hard and yelling at it. He pointed it out to Anara.

Anara was enraged. She stood up in her basket and started yelling. "Stop that! Leave that elephant alone! You're hurting it! Don't you know elephants are very intelligent and deserve to be treated kindly?" Red-faced, Anara vigorously pointed at the man.

Varun looked mortified. "Ma'am, please sit down. That is very dangerous to stand up in that basket." Samal tried to pull her sister back onto the seat. "I too find it quite upsetting that others don't share my respect for these beautiful creatures. But you must not yell. You might frighten my elephants, too."

Anara was mad. She was also embarrassed. But at least she'd tried to tell that other handler what she thought was wrong. Finally, they arrived at the Singh Pole gate. Varun helped Vovó and the kids to get down from Ambara and Bala. He asked for a tip to help feed the elephants. Anara said she'd like to pay for part of the tip with allowance money she'd saved.

As Anara got out her cash, three professional photographers appeared wanting to take their pictures. They chose the least aggressive photographer. All three kids were sad to say goodbye to Ambara and Bala, but it was time. Varun needed to make his way back down the hill for the next run of the day.

There was no doubt that the elephant ride was the highlight of the kids' stay in Jaipur. But Samal also really liked the Sheesh Mahal, or Palace of Mirrors, with its mirror tiles, colored glass and patterned mosaics on the walls and ceiling.

At Ollie's request, they returned the next evening

to see a sound-and-light show at the Amber Fort and Palace. They'd gone to a similar show at the Temple of Karnak in Egypt last fall. The bright lights, Indian folk music, and stories of ancient kings made for an exotic end to their time in the Pink City. On the ride home from the fort, Mom said that more surprises were in store the next day.

A Surprise Visit

"Are you kidding me, Mom? Is this your idea of a surprise?" Anara was looking at Mom's smartphone when she let out a groan—and a string of complaints.

"What are you talking about, Anara?" Mom looked irritated.

"You never said it was nearly a thirteen-hour journey to get to the Valley of Flowers National Park. That's like forever!" Anara shifted in her seat and rolled her eyes with dramatic flair.

Adopting Anara's dramatic mannerisms, Mom said, "Well, my queen, in addition to the fact that your lovely Finnish grandma is taking you hiking through gigantic fields of exotic wildflowers there, I also have a fascinating surprise for you all."

Oliver looked like he had ants in his pants. Samal found herself thinking that it was no wonder that Vovó and Mom got along so well: They both loved

50

surprises, riddles, and mystery novels.

Mom continued, "If you must know, I've been doing my homework, so to speak. I saw that this route to the national park was long. So I checked if any of Pari's relatives lived on the way. It turns out that Pari's uncle Veer lives in a place called Panipat, which is a little less than halfway to the Valley of Flowers. I spoke with Veer and he said he'd be thrilled to host us for a few nights."

"No way! Does he have kids?" Oliver wanted to know.

"Yes, they have three kids, two boys and a girl," Mom said.

Even grouchy-pants Anara was excited by the news of this stopover.

When the Nylunds arrived at the Chaudhuri family's house, Veer greeted them like old friends. He told funny stories about what Pari was like as a toddler and how whenever she came to visit, she ate more kulfi in one sitting than anyone thought was possible. While Samal played with their toddler, Laila, Oliver played soccer in the yard with the Chaudhuri boys, Malik and Pranjal.

Anara decided to help Veer's wife, Roopali, and their servant, Aditi, with the cooking and the shopping. She wanted to learn more about Roopali's vegetarian dishes. The local markets in Panipat weren't nearly as hectic as the ones they visited in Delhi or Jaipur. They picked up the ingredients for eggplant with apple, Punjabi black-eyed peas, cauliflower with spicy yogurt, and some home-style mixed vegetables with lots of spices. Aditi did most of the cooking but Roopali let Anara help with mixing up spices and chopping.

Over their delicious dinner, the twins learned that, like about 80 percent of India's people, the Chaudhuris were Hindu.

"I know Pari's family is Hindu but I don't know much about the religion," Samal admitted.

Veer explained, "I'll just tell you a few things about Hinduism. Unlike many other religions, Hinduism doesn't have a single founder. Many scholars think that Hinduism is the oldest religion in the world. There are lots of Hindu gods and goddesses. And people believe in reincarnation, the idea that a person's soul can be reborn into a new body after death."

Roopali added that Hindus have several interesting holidays. "Speaking of holidays, the day after tomorrow is Independence Day in India. You'll be able to see our local parade and some fireworks too before you leave."

"Cool!" Ollie said.

Before bed, all of the ladies sat in the parlor, enjoying the night breeze and having a last cup of chai. Roopali asked the twins how they came to have such unusual, non-American sounding names. Samal told the story of how Mom and Dad met while they were in the Peace Corps in Kazakhstan. "On the night that they met, they stayed up late talking in a friend's garden. As the early-morning breezes cooled them, they were still chatting and breaking open yet another ripe pomegranate. So when we were born, Mom and Dad decided on the names Anara, meaning 'pomegranate' in Kazakh, and Samal, which means 'breeze'."

Roopali sighed. "I always enjoy hearing love stories. This was a great one to end the night."

Veer offered to bring the kids to his school for a day to see how it compared to school in Queens. The twins couldn't wait. Ollie only agreed to go because he'd be able to spend the day in Malik's class.

As promised, Veer left for school with five kids in tow the next morning. He taught history and was very popular. Students kept coming up to him to say, "Good morning, sir." Many inquired about his guests, wanting to know where the girls and Ollie were from. Veer said they'd find out very soon. Several kids stared at the identical twins with their blonde hair and blue eyes. Some even giggled. Anara and Samal were sort of used to this but they still worried about how the day was going to go.

Embarrassing Moments... and a Black Eye!

Before the school day started, hundreds of kids at Panipat Primary School milled about in the courtyard. Some played ball games, such as catch and handball. Others jumped rope or chatted with their friends. But as soon as the bell rang, all the kids quickly lined up to sing the national anthem. Oliver couldn't get over the name of the anthem, "Jana Gana Mana." The anthem was in a language called Bengali, one of India's many official languages.

After the song was over, Veer stood at the podium in front of the whole school's morning assembly. "Students, I'd like to introduce you to three very special guests, Anara, Samal, and Oliver Nylund. They are here from New York. I know you will make them feel welcome."

Anara and Samal turned pink. They were uncomfortable because a) they were wearing brightly-colored dresses while everyone else wore khaki and white uniforms, and b) being pale-skinned identical twins, they felt a bit like aliens from outer space.

Malik took Ollie to his first grade class. Ollie loved getting to be the star. During morning meeting, the teacher had her students write down questions about life in America for Oliver. He even got to sit at the front of the classroom in the teacher's special chair. And during recess he learned how to play a fun game called kabaddi. The goal of the game was for one team to take over another team's territory without being tagged.

Still feeling a little weird about how everyone was checking them out, Anara and Samal decided to go together to a fifth-grade class. They liked hearing the language during Hindi class. Hindi was another of India's official languages. But Samal was mortified when the music teacher asked them to sing something. Neither of the Nyland girls had an especially stellar voice, in their own opinions. She and Anara decided against The Star Spangled Banner because of its high notes. Instead they sang Row, Row, Row Your Boat and Let It Snow. By the time they got through the two songs, the girls had strawberry-colored cheeks. It was pretty embarrassing.

Anara liked that they got to teach American slang words to the students during English class. If kids in Panipat started saying, "That's dope!" or "What's up?" it would be their doing.

Everything went pretty smoothly until gym class. Neither of the girls played cricket before so all of the Panipat students were excited for them to join in. Anara thought it would be wise to be in the outfield. When one of the boys in the class was at bat, he struck the ball with amazing force. But Samal found herself directly in the line of fire. "OWWWW!!!" she yelled and fell down, hard, onto the ground. The cricket pitch got silent. The teacher ran over to Samal. She was holding her eye and crying. "I can't see, I can't see," she repeated over and over. Anara and the teacher walked Samal down to Veer's classroom.

About ten minutes later, Roopali and Mom showed up. Even though Veer had given Samal an ice pack right away, her eye had already swollen a lot. Roopali phoned her kids' doctor and asked if she could bring Samal in. Luckily, the doctor said yes and took her in right away.

After examining her eye, Dr. Gupta gave Samal lots of advice. "I know your eye is extremely painful right now, Samal, but it doesn't look like there will be any longstanding damage. For the next two days, be sure to put ice packs wrapped in cloth over your eye a few times each day. Then you can apply some warm compresses to increase the blood flow to the tissues around your eye. You can also apply pineapple or papaya around the blackened part of your eye to speed up its healing. Or just eat these fruits. I gave your mom some Arnica ointment to apply a couple times a day. You'll be good as new in a few days if you follow these instructions. No cricket for a while, okay?" He smiled at Samal and sent her on her way.

When Veer got home from work, he apologized for the mishap. Mom told him it was nobody's fault and that these things happen to kids all the time. Anara made Samal feel better by telling her that she got many of the fifth graders' addresses and emails so they could keep in touch.

The last day of their visit was August 15, Independence Day in India. Panipat had a festive atmosphere, with a mid-afternoon parade. They bought Indian flags to wave as the people marched by. Veer treated all the kids to new kites since that was a fun Independence Day tradition. Anara chose a kite that looked like a tropical fish. Samal found a bird-shaped flyer. And Ollie was thrilled with his airplane-themed kite. They ran along a huge soccer field for hours, chasing one another's kites, until they were all wiped out.

Roopali served her family's favorite curry recipe dinner for her guests' last night in Panipat. For dessert she made modak, steamed dumplings containing poppy seeds, coconut, and cardamom. After the meal, the group took a short walk around their neighborhood. Then the ladies sat in the back garden to have a last cup of chai while the boys played a final soccer match. Just before bed, they all watched the fireworks from a hill close to their house.

The next morning, Veer and the boys had to go to school. Everyone hugged and promised that they'd get together in the future. Ollie was really sad to say goodbye to Malik and Pranjal. But Vovó knew what to do. She whispered in his ear, "Dr. Nylund, would you like to be our expedition leader for the next stage of our journey? I've heard it's very remote."

Bumpy Roads and Mountain Challenges

Anara and Samal sat on their hosts' front stoop, waiting for their ride. Sam hated long car trips, especially windy ones. Dad often called her "the Dramamine Queen" because she needed medicine for such rides or she'd throw up. And that was gross for everyone. Especially her fellow passengers in the back seat.

The Valley of Flowers National Park was definitely not the easiest UNESCO site to get to. In fact, after Anara's quick perusal of the maps, she declared it to be "smack dab in the middle of nowhere."

Oliver thought the remote location was cool and adventurous. He informed his sisters, "Vovó said I could be the expedition leader."

Anara groaned. But her sullen mood changed quickly when she saw the lime green Land Rover that pulled up right in front of her. It even had hand-painted mountains on the passenger side door. "Sam, check out this sweet ride! It looks like the Barbie Jeep we had when we were little, doesn't it?"

"It's so cool!" Samal agreed. "Mom said this is the only vehicle to get to Joshimath. If the roads are not washed out from the rains." The Nylund kids introduced themselves to the driver, Arvind. He was very friendly. He said he was excited about the journey since he'd never been to the Valley of Flowers. After loading up the bags, they were off, heading northeast.

The roads were okay at the beginning of the trip, but as they climbed higher and higher, they became more windy and potholed. Even with her medicine, the Dramamine Queen had to have a quick stop by the roadside to vomit. "Ewwww," Oliver said. "Your barf is orange, Sam."

"Shut it, Ollie, or I'll puke on you next time," Samal croaked.

After their quick stop, the kids played games on the ride to pass the time—license plate games, funny place names, I Spy. Anara's favorite town along the way was called Muzaffarnagar. And Samal loved the views in the Motichur Range.

At one point, it looked like they'd reached an impassible section of road. Arvind stopped the Land Rover to assess the situation. Oliver thought this road drama was very exciting. Samal was just grateful for a chance to stop moving and get some fresh air.

"What do we need to do, Arvind?" Ollie asked. He really wanted to help Arvind and some of the other drivers who were stuck.

Arvind smiled. "Well, we must put some boards or logs across the road where the rushing streams have washed it out. But it may take some effort to find enough boards. The road's in pretty bad shape."

Anara, Samal, and Oliver helped poke around the forested area nearby to see if they could find suitable wood chunks. It took a while, with the kids doubling up to carry heavy pieces, but eventually they were able to make a drivable path. "Woohoo!" Ollie shouted. "We did it!"

Arvind and the other drivers thanked the twins and Oliver. Finally the Land Rover was back on its way to the town of Joshimath.

When they arrived, Joshimath wasn't what the

twins had expected. "Sam, this place is rough. Did you see the bathroom? Where's the handle to flush?" Anara said.

"I think we have to pour water from that bucket to flush the toilet," Samal said, pointing at a small blue plastic bucket in the corner. Just then, the lights flickered.

"Yes, girls, this guesthouse is not the Hyatt. The electricity is likely to come on and off without any warning." It was a far stretch from their hotel in New Delhi. Samal was surprised that lots of people wandered around the remote town. Hindu pilgrims passed by. So did hikers with huge backpacks and serious camping gear.

They went into town to buy last-minute supplies for their hiking adventures. Hoping to avoid altitude sickness, since they were at an elevation of 6,000 feet, they made sure to have a little time to rest up in Joshimath before moving on. No one wanted headaches and nausea while hiking in the mountains. At a little restaurant, they drank lots of tea, and ate spicy potatoes —not as spicy as the food in Delhi, which pleased Samal—and flatbread. The girls' job was to stock up on bandages in case of blisters or falls, granola bars, and bottled water for the hikes. They felt very grown-up buying supplies on their own with the local currency.

Unfortunately, no one slept well in Joshimath. The blankets at the guesthouse were scratchy and it was cold at night. Even in her pajamas, a fleece, and socks, Anara shivered all night long.

The ride from Joshimath to Govind Ghat was slow the next morning. It was only 21 miles but they had to repeatedly stop for mules crossing the road. "My goodness, how many mules live here?" Samal wondered aloud. "And who are all these people walking in groups? I thought we were in the middle of nowhere."

Anara said, "Don't forget, Sam, India has over a billion people. Nowhere is going to be completely empty. It's a little like New York in that way."

Arvind told them that lots of the walkers were pilgrims traveling from one religious site to another.

Anara continued, "By the way, everyone, you know how I don't like heights? Well, you should all appreciate that I'm trying hard to ignore the

Alaknanda River thundering below us. This road doesn't even have guardrails."

Just two days earlier, a landslide had completely closed off stretches of road between Joshimath and Govind Ghat. Arvind crept along. Even Oliver was wondering to himself if the vehicle would make it.

Trekking and Triumph

"I thought that was supposed to be an hour's drive," Samal complained. Arvind smiled, unoffended. They'd had to go off-roading several times to make it to Govind Ghat. The Land Rover, once a beautiful shade of green, was now completely splattered with mud. But at least they'd arrived. Unfortunately, the slow ride meant that they had to hurry onto the trail to Ghangaria. That was where they'd be staying for the night.

Oliver was confused. "I thought we were seeing the Valley of the Flowers. Where are we going now?"

Never easily flustered, Vovó explained the plans. "Here's the thing, Ollie. We need to hire some mules and guides to take us to our next stop, Ghangaria. It's an eight-mile hike from where we are now to Ghangaria. The trail is steep and narrow. It will take between four and eight hours, depending on our pace. We need to get there before dark. Tonight we'll stay in the little village of

Ghangaria and tomorrow we'll hike through the Valley of the Flowers. Does that make sense?"

Oliver, Samal, and Anara all nodded. They appreciated knowing what was coming next.

With their blond hair and colorful trekking outfits, the Nylund kids attracted attention. Vovó hired two mule-waalas and one porter, called a pitthoo. One of the mule-walaas brought his son Fakeer who was about the twins' age. The porter and the mules carried all the baggage. None of the people helping them were really chatty. But Anara wondered if that was just because everyone was paying attention to their footing.

The group departed Govind Ghat, crossing a footbridge over the Lakshmana River. The trail was littered with mule dung. Avoiding the poop was impossible. The twins figured they'd just have clean their hiking boots after the trip.

Anara was curious. "Are all these hikers heading to the Valley of the Flowers, Vovó?"

"No, love. Many of them are going to a lake called Hemkund Sahib. It's considered holy by some Indian people."

After a particularly steep stretch of trail, they stopped

at a little stall for snacks and tea. Samal was thrilled to eat some chips and ramen-style noodles.

"My feet hurt, Vovó. These hiking boots are not very comfortable," Ollie grumped. "I think I have some blisters."

"Let's see, Oliver." Vovó pulled off his socks.

"Ow! That kills! I think you just took some of my skin off with the socks. Stupid hiking socks!"

After removing his socks, Vovó confirmed that Ollie's suspicions were right. He did have several fiery looking blisters. She patched his feet with ointment and bandages. "How about you ride one of the mules for a while, Oliver, and give your tootsies a break?"

"Okay," he said.

Along the way, the girls took photos of Bhyundaar village. Nestled into the mountains, the village was beautiful. The Lakshmana River flowed right through it. Samal noted how fast the river's current flowed. She was glad she didn't have to swim in it. The twins snapped lots of the exotic flowers blooming off the trail. Their porter knew the English names of all the flowers. Oliver especially liked the Inula and the Himalayan whorlflower.

The kids cheered when they came across a stone marker that read Ghangaria: 1 kilometer. Anara saw a helipad and asked, "How much does it cost to take a helicopter here? Who does that?"

"Helicopter travel up here is expensive. It's really only the very rich who have organized tours or who aren't in shape to hike that take helicopters here," their grandmother said. "But they miss the scenery along the way, and the sense of accomplishment at the end of a long, strenuous hike."

"They don't get blisters that way," Ollie noted.

Samal quipped, "Yeah, they also miss tons of poop and almost running off the side of a cliff to avoid oncoming mules." She'd had a bit of a run-in with a mule driver coming down from Ghangaria. The kids now understood that you had to move in toward the hill-side of the path, not the slope-side, when making room for animals.

By the time they arrived in the little village of Ghangaria, the kids were all bone-tired. Ollie reveled in how nice it felt to take off his heavy hiking boots. Everyone took some time to unwind before getting dinner. Their little bungalow was cute and simple, and the heat worked better than in Govind Ghat.

All of the restaurants along the village's main passage had similar menus. So the kids decided on one of the closest ones to where they were staying. Oliver and the girls drew with crayons on their paper placemats. They didn't say much during the meal. Everyone inhaled the chicken curry and chana masala, a chickpea in tomato sauce dish. A quick round of Yahtzee ended the night. Anara guessed some Western hiker must have left the game behind.

After a better night's sleep, expedition leader Oliver was ready for adventure. Even with his blistered feet, he managed to walk at a decent clip. It was only about two miles between Ghangaria and the start of the main valley where the flowers were located. They hired a wildlife expert to accompany them for the day. Vovó said, "Wasn't it Samal who called me a 'bird nerd'?"

Samal chuckled, "Yeah, that was me when we went to Acadia."

Chetna was their wilderness guide for the day. A graduate student at Cornell University, Chetna was spending a semester leading tourists around the national park that she'd grown up near. She enjoyed answering the kids' questions about the plants and animals in the Valley. Anara said that the scene–and the woolly white Edelweiss flowers–reminded her a little of the movie *The Sound of Music*.

Chetna taught Oliver how to focus her binoculars on birds in the trees. He was thrilled to see a Himalayan musk deer in the distance. Samal took photos of a yellow-bellied fantail flycatcher. The Nylunds loved walking through clumps of wildflowers up to their knees. They came in many different colors–pinks, purples, yellows, and more. They took hundreds of photos but Ollie said his favorite was the Himalayan Blue Poppy.

It was a merry band of hikers that returned to their bungalow that evening. Mom met them for dinner in Ghangaria. She brought some presents from her UNESCO colleagues to dinner. Oliver loved the Valley of Flowers National Park patch for his backpack and the stuffed animal of a Himalayan deer.

"Girls, you'll have to wait for your present because it's being shipped to the Delhi offices tomorrow," Mom said. "But trust me, it's a surprise worth waiting for."

Street Children and Namaste (Goodbye), India!

Two days of hiking left the kids with sore legs but proud spirits. All three Nylunds had gotten to ride on mules in the Himalayas. But they were glad that their mode of transportation back to Delhi was Arvind's Land Rover.

Not surprisingly, part of the nearly nine-hour journey was a snooze fest for Ollie, Samal, and Anara. But Samal had other things on her mind. She was curious about Fakeer, the son of the mule-waala. "Mom, how come Fakeer wasn't at school? Or those kids at the train station in New Delhi? Don't kids all go to school here?"

Mom sighed. "Not all kids have the same luxury of education that you do. I know it may sound weird that education is a luxury. But around the world, many kids don't get the chance. Their families need them to work, to earn money, and to help in the fields.

76

Two days of hiking left the kids with sore legs but proud spirits. All three Nylunds had gotten to ride on mules in the Himalayas. But they were glad that their mode of transportation back to Delhi was Arvind's Land Rover.

Not surprisingly, part of the nearly nine-hour journey was a snooze fest for Ollie, Samal, and Anara. But Samal had other things on her mind. She was curious about Fakeer, the son of the mule-waala. "Mom, how come Fakeer wasn't at school? Or those kids at the train station in New Delhi? Don't kids all go to school here?"

Mom sighed. "Not all kids have the same luxury of education that you do. I know it may sound weird that education is a luxury. But around the world, many kids don't get the chance. Their families need them to work, to earn money, and to help in the fields. Some families cannot afford the school uniforms that are required. Others live far from schools. I'm sure Fakeer's dad would like to be able to send his son to school. But maybe during the busy season of tourists visiting the Valley of Flowers, he needs Fakeer's help too much."

"Why didn't Fakeer say anything to us?" Ollie wanted to know. "I wanted to talk to him."

"Perhaps he felt embarrassed. He might not have spoken English very well. Or he may have been trained by his dad not to talk to the customers. It's hard to say," Mom answered. "One of the reasons I wanted you kids to come on this trip was to see what an amazing country India is. But I also wanted you to see how fortunate you are compared to so many kids around the world."

"That makes me feel sad. Is there any way we can help kids here?" Anara asked.

"Sure enough, before leaving India, you'll learn more about kids' lives in India. We'll give some money to an organization called Salaam Balaak. For the moment, enjoy the scenery on the ride back to Delhi."

The kids were happy to get back to their hotel in Delhi. Samal said that the hot shower was one of the nicest she'd ever had.

On their last day in Delhi, Ollie and his sisters went on a walking tour of Delhi run by Salaam Baalak. They met their guide Jahi at the southern end of the railway station in New Delhi in a part of the city called Paharganj. Jahi told the group a little about himself. "I started living on the streets of New Delhi when I was about eight. My father died and my mother could not afford to feed all five of us kids. I gradually met other kids my age that also lived on the streets. Some left home because of abuse. Others had reasons like mine. But everyone, including myself, hoped for a better life on our own."

As Jahi led them around the railway station and out onto some of Paharganj's narrow back alleys, he talked about different ways that kids tried to survive and make a living on their own. He said he couldn't really feed or clothe himself properly, but was lucky that people from Salaam Baalak discovered him. At first, he went to the charity's main office during the day. There he made friends, got hot meals, and took some basic educational classes. After a while, when a space opened up, he was able to stay in a boys' shelter.

Eventually, Jahi said he was reunited with his mother and siblings. He started giving tours for Salaam Baalak and was able to help support his family. At the end of the tour, the Nylunds visited the charity's main office. They met about a dozen children between the ages of five and thirteen. Together they played games and the twins learned some Bollywood dance moves. Anara and Samal also taught the kids in the office some of their dance moves—they took African dance and hip hop classes. When the twins danced, all their new Indian friends clapped and joined along. When the tour was over, Ollie and his sisters took money from their wallets to make a donation.

That night, Samal wrote in her journal about her experiences of meeting Jahi and the other kids. She mentioned how she had some moments where she thought she might cry but that she bit the inside of her cheeks and tried to focus on what Jahi was telling her. She wrote that she would like to try to donate some of her allowance money more often to charities that help educate kids around the world.

On the plane back from Indira Gandhi International Airport the next evening, Mom told the girls that their surprise had arrived. Anara opened her package first. "No way! A real churidar suit, and

it's even orange and hot pink! Where did you get this?"

"My colleague from the Valley of Flowers said that no young ladies should leave India without a churidar suit. Apparently, people here have their tailors make the suits to fit them exactly. So I told her your American sizes and the tailor made these with your favorite colors. Do you like yours, Sam?"

"Purple leggings and a purple and gold print tunic, I love it! I can't wait to wear it to school and show Pari." Samal beamed. "And, Mom, if you ever have another work trip you want to let us tag along for, I'm totally game!"

Anara and Oliver agreed.

Samal's Travel Journal

I'm waiting by the gate to catch our flight home from Indira Gandhi International Airport. It's been pretty busy the last couple of weeks and I'm afraid that if I don't get a little more in my journal, I'll forget all the awesome things I saw and did in India. Visiting the Chaudhuris was great—Roopali made the best food. She wrote out her favorite coconut burfi recipe for me. Here it is!

Saffron Coconut Burfi

Ingredients
$1/4$ cup hot water
1 tablespoon saffron powder
3 tablespoons butter
1 14-ounce can sweetened condensed milk
4 cups dried coconut
1 teaspoon ground cardamom

Directions

1. Dissolve the saffron powder in hot water and set aside.

2. Melt the butter in a medium saucepan over medium heat, then add the sweetened condensed milk and the desiccated coconut. Stir until the mixture reaches an even consistency.

3. Divide the mixture into two equal parts. Add the saffron water to one part, mixing it well. In a separate bowl, add the cardamom to the other part and mix well.

4. Place the cardamom-coconut mixture into the bottom of a square dish (like an 8x8-inch pan). Flatten until the mixture is pretty smooth on top. Then place the saffron-coconut mixture on top of the cardamom-coconut mixture and flatten.

5. Place the dish into the fridge to cool for one hour before cutting the layered Burfi into desired shapes.

At Veer's school, Mrs. Singh asked me to compare America and India. I told the class about trick-or-treating on Halloween and the foods we eat for Thanksgiving. Mrs. Singh's class told me all kinds of things I didn't know about India. Here's some of what I discovered:

Fun Facts about India

Capital: New Delhi

Official Languages: English, Hindi, Bengali, Telugu, Marathi, Tamil, Urdu, Gujarati, Malayalam, Kannada, Oriya, Punjabi, Assamese, Kashmiri, Sindhi, Sanskrit

Population: 1,236,344,631 (July 2014 estimate)

Famous People: Mohandas Gandhi (1869-1948), Indira Gandhi (1917-1984); Ravi Shankar (1920-2012)

Holidays Celebrated: Republic Day (January26); Independence Day (August 15); Mahatma Gandhi's birthday (October 2); Many Indians also celebrate Hindu holidays such as Holi and Diwali

Climate: varies from temperate in the north to a tropical monsoon climate in the south

Significant Events

c. 3000 BCE – Indus River valley civilization begins to develop.

c. 700s CE – Muslims arrive in India.

1526-1857 – India is ruled by the Mughal Empire.

1858 – India officially becomes part of the British Empire as a British colony.

1920 – Mohandas (Mahatma) Gandhi starts nonviolent protests against British rule.

1947 – India gains independence from Britain; India and Pakistan go to war over the territory of Kashmir.

1948 – Mohandas Gandhi is assassinated.

1966 – Indira Gandhi becomes the first female prime minister of India.

2000 – India's billionth citizen is born.

I really liked listening to sitar music in Mrs. Singh's class. I'd never heard of a sitar–it's a stringed instrument that some people call an Indian lute. Ravi Shankar was a famous Indian sitar player who worked with the Beatles and helped popularize Indian music around the world.

Arvind told me about some of the Hindu holidays. I'd love to come back for *Holi*. This holiday celebrates the beginning of spring. But on *Holi*, people throw brightly colored powder at each other. It looks like so much fun!

I really liked visiting the Pink City of Jaipur. Even the city's tourist map was pink. So cool!

I would have liked to see what the landscape around the Amber Fort looked like back when it was built in the late 1500s. I imagine a steep hillside with bushes growing here and there. I loved the "Magic Flower" fresco there, carved out of marble. Here are some snapshots I took:

Amber Fort

"Magic Flower" fresco

The elephant ride was definitely exciting! Veer told me that elephants have been domesticated in India for a long time. Some even work in forests to help move tree trunks. Others are used in ceremonies and festivals. Roopali's boys told me that India is home to tons of animals, from tigers to cobras! I'm sure glad I didn't run into any of them. I did see some beautiful swallowtail butterflies and many neat birds. My absolute favorite was the Indian ringneck parakeet. Here's a photo:

Indian ringneck parakeet

Discussion Questions

1. How is life in India today similar to your own life? How is it different?

2. India is a huge country with many different climates and landforms. Which areas do you think are best for farming and why?

3. If you could talk to any historical figure from India's past, who would it be and what would you like to ask him or her?

4. How has Indian life changed from the days of the Indus River valley civilization to today?

5. If you had the chance to travel to India, where would you most want to visit and why?

6. Compare the food that people eat in India to the food you eat at home.

Vocabulary

Do you remember these words from the book? Can you define them? Try using each in a sentence, then mix up the sentences to make a funny, jumbled-up story!

altitude
cardamom
deity
Hindi
intrigued
Koran
monsoon
mortified
mosque
outskirts
pomegranate
reincarnation
rickshaw
saffron
subtly

Websites to Visit

Learn more about the landmarks, traditions, and people of India:

www.timeforkids.com/destination/india/day-in-life

http://kids.nationalgeographic.com/content/kids/en_US/explore/countries/india

http://teacher.scholastic.com/activities/globaltrek/destinations/india.htm

About the Author:

From jellybeans to vampires, Alicia Klepeis loves to research fun and out-of-the-ordinary topics that make nonfiction exciting for readers. Alicia began her career at the National Geographic Society. She is the author of several kids' books, including *Africa, Understanding Saudi Arabia Today*, and *The World's Strangest Foods*. Her first picture book, *Francisco's Kites*, came out in May 2015. She has also written dozens of articles in magazines such as National Geographic Kids, Kiki, and FACES. Alicia is currently working on a middle-grade novel, as well as several projects involving international food, American history, and world cultures. She lives with her family in upstate New York.

About the Illustrator:

Simon Abbott has been illustrating children's books for 15 years. He specializes in bold colors and delightful characters of all kinds and describes his work as fun, fresh and happy. His easy style has instant appeal and helps to communicate complex ideas and concepts in an instant. Whether he is drawing playground fun, astronauts, dinosaurs or monkeys swinging through trees, his art is always engaging and is guaranteed to make children smile. Simon lives and works in Suffolk, England, with his partner Sally, and 3 boys called Jack, Nathan and Alfie.